"I WILL TAKE THE LEAD," WHISPERED RIATHA, "FOR ELVEN EYES COPE WELL WITH GLOOM." And into the dark environs of Baron Stoke's fortress they crept, Riatha's gleaming sword in hand, the others following, bringing up the rear. "Which way?" whispered Riatha, confronted with the choice of labyrinthine paths and winding stairs. But the answer was cut off by a distant, tortured scream.

Down a long series of steps, towards the sound, they plunged. And at the bottom, Vulgs came at them out of the darkness; great, black wolf-like creatures, their yellow eyes glowing. Behind them came dark, scimitar-bearing Rucks, goblin-like with their spindly legs and pointed, wide-gapped teeth. And suddenly, something glittering flew through the air and shattered on the stairwell wall. Thick green fumes wooshed forth, and they were all falling down an endless, spiraling tunnel. . . .

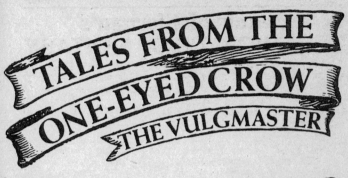

TALES FROM THE ONE-EYED CROW
THE VULGMASTER

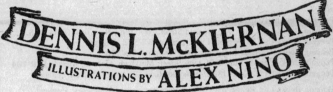

DENNIS L. McKIERNAN
ILLUSTRATIONS BY ALEX NINO

Script Adaptation by David Keller

Lettering by Kurt Hathaway

A BYRON PREISS BOOK

A ROC BOOK

NEW AMERICAN LIBRARY

A DIVISION OF PENGUIN BOOKS USA INC., NEW YORK

ROC

Published by the Penguin Group

Penguin Books USA Inc., 375 Hudson Street, New York, New York 10014, U.S.A.

Penguin Books Ltd, 27 Wrights Lane, London W8 5TZ, England

Penguin Books Australia Ltd, Ringwood, Victoria, Australia

Penguin Books Canada Ltd, 2801 John Street, Markham, Ontario, Canada L3R 1B4

Penguin Books (N.Z.) Ltd, 182-190 Wairau Road, Auckland 10, New Zealand

Penguin Books Ltd, Registered Offices: Harmondsworth, Middlesex, England

First published by Roc, an imprint of New American Library, a division of Penguin Books USA Inc.

Published simultaneously in Canada.

First printing, July, 1991

10 9 8 7 6 5 4 3 2

 **Roc is a trademark of New American Library,
a division of Penguin books USA Inc.**

Printed in Canada

Cover painting by Alex Nino

Cover design by Alex Jay

Book design by Steve Brenninkmeyer

Lettering by Kurt Hathaway

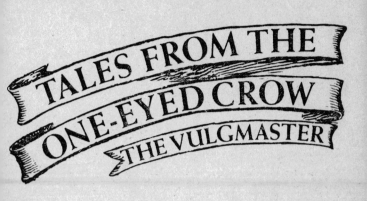

TALES FROM THE
ONE-EYED CROW
THE VULGMASTER

Prologue
by Dennis McKiernan

Long, long ago, when the world was a younger and much more mystical and magical place, there existed a strange and wonderful Folk, Folk of all type and nature, Folk of light and air and crystal and clear water, of forest and green, and of heat and sand and soaring red stone, of clover and field and growing grain . . . and more.

Oh, yes, more . . . much more.

Too, there were creatures of the night, of the dark; some sinister and cruel, though not all, for night oft comes gently unto the soul.

These were days when Faerie and the world were one, when magic was real, when great quests were undertaken, and mighty deeds were done.

And common folk gathered in the taverns and about hearths and in the great rooms of faraway castles, around the cook fires and in chambers delved from stone, in caverns, in forest glades, and elsewhere, to listen to the tales of these mighty deeds, of these great quests, listeners rapt in the tale teller's words.

Bards and Loremasters, storytellers and singers, minstrels and chanters and aged wise ones; these were the bearers on the tales, though occasionally some were written down for any and all to read, given that they knew how.

Yet whether or not people could read, still they depended upon the tale weavers to amaze and startle them, to enchant them with stories of fable and wonder, to cause them to look over their shoulders into the shadows to see if aught was creeping up on them in the dark.

And in a place called Mithgar, in the land of the Boskydells, in the village of Woody Hollow, there in one of the Seven Dells, in a tiny tavern known as the One-Eyed Crow, there often could be found one special tale teller, well known among his Kind.

He lived in Woody Hollow, among the Folk of this Land, a Folk known as Warrows. They are a shy Folk, not often seen, unless they wish to be. Wee Folk, you would call them—slender and graceful and elfinlike, standing between three and four feet tall when fully grown. And they have pointed ears and large tilted jewellike eyes, magnificent eyes, with deep glints and sparkles, eyes of three colors only, sapphire blue, emerald green, and amber gold.

And this tale teller: Gaffer Tom, they called him, an eld Warrow, a granther buccan, who would sit in his customary corner of the Crow and sip his ale and puff on his pipe and spin yarns long into the night.

From miles about, they would come to hear him. And he never disappointed them.

Though he was a person of Warrow renown, still, not many knew him; not many knew Gaffer Tom's own tale, where he'd come from, how he'd got there, or even a thing or two that he had done in his youth.

Yet one day they caught a glimmer of the truth, for on that day, withour warning, a blizzard blew down upon the Boskydells, a blizzard so fierce that it trapped people wherever they happened to be. And down at the One-Eyed Crow. . .

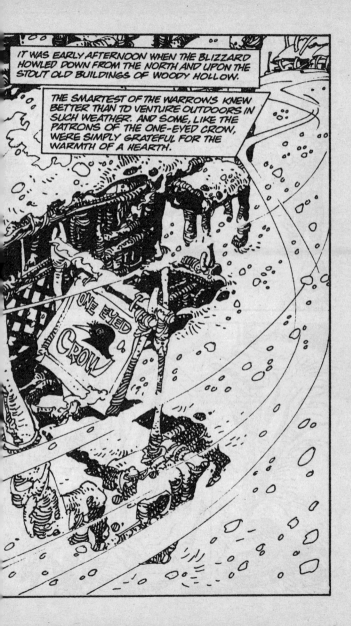

IT WAS EARLY AFTERNOON WHEN THE BLIZZARD HOWLED DOWN FROM THE NORTH AND UPON THE STOUT OLD BUILDINGS OF WOODY HOLLOW.

THE SMARTEST OF THE WARROWS KNEW BETTER THAN TO VENTURE OUTDOORS IN SUCH WEATHER. AND SOME, LIKE THE PATRONS OF THE ONE-EYED CROW, WERE SIMPLY GRATEFUL FOR THE WARMTH OF A HEARTH.

ONE EYED CROW

WE WERE OUT IN THE OPEN. WE LOOKED FOR HOURS FOR SHELTER. A STAND OF TREES, THE LEE OF A CLIFF... ANYTHING!

BUT THEN THE DARKNESS FELL... AND WITH IT AN AWFUL FEELING OF VULNERABILITY.

THAT'S WHEN THEY ATTACKED. VULGS, AND TWENTY OR MORE RUCKS... HURLING OUT OF THE SNOW TOWARD US LIKE BLACK GHOSTS.

THE THREE SET FORTH IN THE DARKNESS, HEADING NORTHWARD UP THE VALLEY, THE STORM WANING AS THEY MADE THEIR WAY TOWARD THE BARON'S CASTLE. THEY WERE VIGILANT IN THEIR WATCH, FOR EVERY STEP BROUGHT THEM CLOSER TO THEIR QUARRY... AND THE UNKNOWN.

HE GATHERED A SMALL FORCE FROM AMONG MY KINDRED AND SET THEM OUT THROUGH THE WOODS.

HE LURED THEM INTO THE CAVES, THOSE IN THE GRIMWALLS JUST SOUTH OF THE CRESTAN PASS.

NOW IT IS TIME FOR REST.
BUT WHY?. WE'LL NEVER MAKE IT AT THIS PACE. PETAL...SHE MIGHT BE IN...
ARGUE NOT WITH ME, PEBBLE, FOR I WOULD HAVE THEE ARRIVE AT STOKE'S HOLT WITH ENOUGH STRENGTH TO WHIRL THY SLING.

AND SO, THROUGHOUT THE DAY, THE COMRADES RESTED, AND STOOD WATCH IN TURN.

IT WAS NEAR DUSK WHEN THEY TOOK UP THE TREK ONCE AGAIN.

THEY CAME WITHIN SIGHT OF THE STRONGHOLT JUST ERE MIDNIGHT. THE FULL MOON LIT THE GIGANTIC TURRET AS IF IT WERE MADE OF OBSIDIAN.

AT TIMES THE ELFESS COULD NOT FIND A HOLD SUITABLE FOR PEBBLE'S SHORT STATURE. URUS WOULD HAVE TO GIVE HIM A BOOST.

AND THOUGH HIS HAND WAS STRONG AND STEADY, PEBBLE HAD NOTHING BUT AIR TO GRASP AS HE WAS LIFTED UPWARD, AND HE BIT HIS LIP IN TERROR.

HURRY!
HOLD TIGHT, PEBBLE. I'M COMING!
GRASP HERE AND CLIMB TO THAT LEDGE ABOVE. THERE YOU CAN REST AND GATHER YOUR WITS.

THE TWO BELOW WOULD NEED ALL OF RIATHA'S STRENGTH TO MAKE IT ONTO THE LANDING.

THROUGH THE DARKENED
ROOM THEY PASSED,
WEAPONS AT THE
READY...

PEBBLE NEARLY STUMBLED DOWN A STAIRWELL IN HIS EFFORT TO FIND THE SOURCE OF THE TORTURED SCREAMS. BUT URUS AND RIATHA WERE RIGHT BEHIND.

URUS WAS THE FIRST TO SENSE THAT THEY WERE BEING WATCHED. BUT WHAT THE LANTERN LIT AHEAD OF THEM WERE NOT HUMAN EYES.

LOOK AHEAD... THERE...!

AN ARCANE GAS BILLOWED OUT FROM STOKE'S SHATTERED SPHERE AND ALL THREE FELL SENSELESS.

WHEN PEBBLE CAME TO AGAIN, THERE WAS A FAMILIAR VOICE CALLING TO HIM; IT WAS THE VOICE OF HIS BELOVED.

TOMMY! TOMMY... WAKE UP!

TOMLIN'S SHOT WAS TRUE, AND RIATHA'S GRIM SMILE CONVEYED HER THANKS.

THE FIGHT RAGED ON FOR MANY MINUTES, AND FOR A TIME IT SEEMED THAT THE RUCKS MIGHT RETREAT.

BUT STOKE WAS NOT YET DONE. THE VULG LET OUT A MIGHTY HOWL WHICH ECHOED THROUGHOUT THE MASSIVE HOLT.

TOMLIN WAS QUICK TO REGAIN HIS FEET... THE VULGS WERE NOW SHUT OUT.

RIATHA! SWIFT! TO THE BALCONY!

GRIMLY, THEY STRODE TOWARD THE BALCONY, DEATH FOR STOKE IN THEIR EYES. YET THROUGH THE HALLS OF THE HOLT, THEY COULD HEAR THE IRONSHOD TREAD OF RUCKS MARCHING, COMING TO RELEASE THE VULGS.

...AND OUT ON THE BALCONY, THE PAIR WATCHED AS THE BATTLE RAGED, AFRAID TO STRIKE FOR FEAR OF HITTING URUS.

THE VULG'S POISON FLOWED THROUGH THE GREAT BEAR'S VEINS, AND URUS KNEW HE HAD NOT THE STRENGTH LEFT TO CRUSH HIS FOE. AND HE KNEW HE WAS FALLING UNTO DEATH FROM THE VENOM.

YET WITH THE LAST OF HIS STRENGTH, URUS HURLED THE BLACK CREATURE OUTWARD, SENDING THE MONSTER HOWLING TO THE VALLEY BELOW.

AAAOOO!

THEN IT CHANGED AGAIN INTO SOMETHING WINGED AND BLACK, AND IT SOARED THROUGH THE VALLEY AS IF PURSUED.

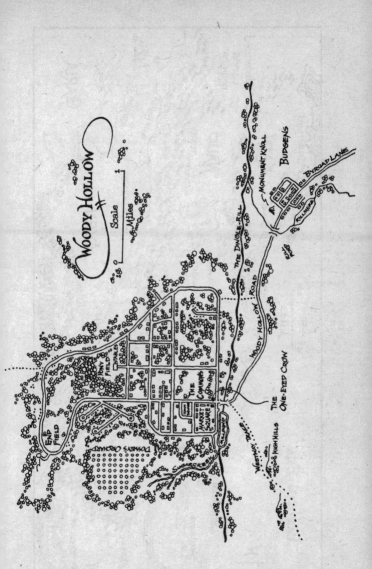

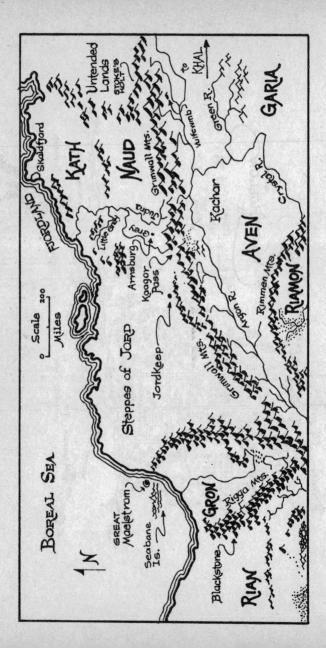

Weapons
Riatha's Sword

It is known that Riatha's sword was forged in Duellin, a city in lost Atala. Its maker was Dwynfor, the greatest Elven smith upon Mithgar, who gave it to Riatha's mother, Rein, who after a long and faithful Guardianship upon Mithgar, gave the weapon to her daughter, Riatha.

Housed in a green scabbard with a tooled harness suitable for strapping over the shoulder or girting about the waist, with a blade and pommel and crossguard of rare dark starsilver and a grip inlaid with pale jade crosshatched for firm grasp, the sword is a "special" weapon. It has a truename, a name which when invoked has a terrible effect upon those about, but what this truename and effect are is not known to this researcher at this time.

Pebble's Sling

Pebble's sling and slingstones are common and of no special material. However, after the events described herein, Dwarven smiths forged special silver bullets for Tomlin's sling, patterned somewhat after the silver bob given to him by Molly in Vulfcwmb.

Petal's Knives

Petal's steel throwing knives are the marvelously balanced set of ten once owned by her sire. After the events of this tale, she wore them in a pair of bandoliers crossed over her torso, five to a belt. Dwarven smiths forged a pair of silver throwing knives for her, which she also bore in her bandoliers.

Urus's Morning Star

The ball and chain on Urus's morning star are simply made of high-quality steel, and the haft is of black oak. For most Men it is a two-handed weapon, but Urus's strength is such that he ordinarily wields it with but one hand.

Elves

Elves are one of the immortal Folk of Adonar, the High World. Some live on Mithgar, the Mid World. Elves are made up of two strains: the Lian and the (slightly smaller) Dylvana. In general, the adults range in height from four and one half feet to five and one half feet, though some are as much as six feet tall. Tilted eyes. Pointed ears. Slim. Agile. Swift. Sharp-sensed. Reserved. Forest dwellers. Artisans.

Because Elves are immortal, they have learned to live in a manner to preserve and protect the earth. Too, they have discovered that the truly worthwhile things concern hearth and home and simple pleasures.

Immortality also leads to the mastering of many skills, for each Elf has millennia to learn the arts and crafts which interest him or her. Beyond being skillful in everyday crafts, Elves tend to take up the creative arts: music, silversmithing, jewelry, art, poetry, song, dance, tale telling, and so forth. Too, they are quite skillful in the ways of nature, in the healing arts, in the ways of the sea and of the road, in languages, as well as in many, many other

areas of life and living. After all, they have forever to learn.

Some Elves are said to have mastered the ways of magic, though they profess not to know what is meant by that term. Nevertheless, Elven-forged weapons are marvelous, many having special capabilities. It is also known that when dying—by violence, accident, exposure, or by rare sickness—an Elf can by some means project his or her final thoughts unto another Elf, usually a close kindred. This projection is known as Death Rede, and it is a traumatic blow unto the recipient of the rede; for Elves are immortal, and for one to die means that a virtually unthinkable event has occured to a loved one. A Death Rede is the final message of the dying Elf, and it often contains visions as well as the Elf's last words.

The Lian are also known as the Guardians of Mithgar. The Dylvana are also known as the Wood Elves. Both speak a native tongue known as Sylva.

Warrows

Warrows are a wee folk, the adults ranging between three and four feet tall. They have peculiar eyes, large, tilted, and jewellike. There eyes come in three hues only: sapphire blue, emerald green, and amber gold. It has been said that Warrow eyes can see a range of colors that no other Folk can.

Except for their gemlike eyes and their short stature, in all other respects Warrows appear to be Elves, including pointed ears. However, unlike Elves, Warrows are mortal, and barring accident or disease, most Warrows live to be 100 years old, and many reach the age of 120 years.

They are deft and quick, and can move virtually without making noise. And given the slightest cover, they can conceal themselves from searching eyes. They speak a native language known as Twyll.

Warrows are found on most of the major land masses of Mithgar, and they come in all skin colors: white, yellow, red, brown, black, and the hues between.

Male Warrows are called buccen (singular: buccan), and females are called dammen (singular: damman).

Baeron (singular: Baeran)

Baeron are Men of great stature and strength living in the northern vales of the river Argon and in the Greatwood and in the forest of Darda Erynian (also known as the Great Greenhall and as the Blackwood of old) on Mithgar. The adult males range in height from six to seven feet, and the females from five feet eight inches to six feet six inches.

Legand has it that many Baeron speak the language of Wolves or Bears or both, and that some can shapechange into these (and perhaps other) beasts; this is probably myth, though some of the tales do seen rather reliable.

The Baeron are wise in the ways of woodcraft, and despite their bulk, move swiftly and silently through the woods. They are excellent hunters and foragers, and seem to have mastered swimming, climbing, stalking, hiding, and many other outdoor skills.

Their native tongue is Baeron, though they oft communicate with one another using bird calls and animal sounds, and silent hand signals.

Rucks

Rucks are evil, goblinlike creatures from Neddra, the Under World, who came to Mithgar before the Sundering, when the ways between the Planes were still open. They are four to five feet tall. Dark skinned. They have wide-gapped, pointed teeth. Bat-wing ears. They are skinny-armed, bandylegged. Rucks are unskilled in arts and crafts and weaponry.

Although unskilled in combat, Rucks overwhelm their foe by sheer numbers.

Rucks suffer the Ban, whithering into dust if they are exposed to sunlight.

Rucks speak Sluk, their native tongue, although a very few also speak the Common Tongue.

Also known as Rukha by the Elves, Rutcha by the Baeron, Goblins by the Men of Valon, and as Ukhs by the Dwarves.

Vulgs

Vulgs are large, black, wolflike creatures, some nearly as large as a pony. They have a virulent bite—perhaps poison, perhaps a swift-acting form of rabies— which prevents the clotting of blood and eventually causes the victim to fall into foam-flecked madness. Vulg bites are treatable by Gwynthyme (a rare golden mint) poultice, or by exposure of the victim to sunlight.

Vulgs suffer the Ban and will whither to dust if exposed to sunlight. Vulgs act as scouts and trackers for the Foul Folk, in addition to being savage ravers.

Also known as the Vulpen in the Sluk Tongue.

Tomlin

A slim, buccan Warrow, Tomlin is three feet four inches high and has red hair and eyes of emerald green.

Tomlin was born "on the road," and knew no other life than that of a travelling entertainer. His sire was a minstrel—lutes, flutes, and harps—and Tomlin played a drum. Tomlin's dam accompanied them on the road as a singer, and as a tightrope walker; too, she acted in the dramas they staged, as did all members of the troupe. Tomlin's dam educated her wee buccan and Petal in reading, writing, and ciphering.

The buccan became most proficient with a sling, often hunting game for members of the sideshow troupe. As a game hunter, Tomlin also became an excellent tracker, and learned well the arts of stalking and hiding, something which comes rather easily to a Warrow.

Tomlin was 23 when his sire and dam were slain by Baron Stoke.

Tomlin is also known as Pebble, because of the slingstones he carries. His full name is Tomlin Fenn.

Riatha

One of the immortal Lian, Riatha came to Mithgar some three hundred or so years before the Sundering. Standing some five feet six inches tall, slender, graceful Riatha has pale golden hair, and her eyes are silver grey.

A trained warrior, she participated in the War of the Ban as part of a band of Lian Guardians opposing Gyphon and his lieutenant, Modru.

In the four thousand years following the War of the Ban and prior to the events related in *The Vulgmaster*, Riatha became proficient in many, many arts and crafts and skills.

Some three years past, Riatha was whelmed to her knees by the Death Rede of her brother, Talar, who was flayed alive and then impaled by Baron Stoke.

Riatha's actual age is unknown, but no matter what it is, she is just at the beginning of an immortal life.

Urus

A giant bear of a man, Urus is six feet eight inches high. He has dark reddish brown hair, lighter at the tips, giving it a silvery grizzled look. His face is covered with a close-cropped full beard of the same grizzled brown. His eyes are a dark amber.

Urus is one of the so-called "Cursed Ones," a shapechanger, able to transform into a large bear. Before he began pursuing Baron Stoke, Urus was Chieftain of the Baeron Men at the hands of Baron Stoke.

Like all Baeron, Urus is an excellent woodsman, with surpassing hunting, tracking, stalking, hiding, and other woodsman's skills.

Urus was 40 when Baron Stoke slew Urus's comrades.

Stoke

Stoke is said to be the son of a Baron, though some claim that he was actually the son born from the unholy mating of a daemon summoned up by Baron Stoke's mother. It is claimed that the Baroness, upon hearing of the death of her husband in a hunting accident, made a pact with a daemon to impregnate her so that she could claim she was carrying the unborn child of the slain Baron, hence, could maintain her claim on the Baron's estates.

In any event, the story goes that when Stoke was born, his mouth was fang-filled, and as a result he suckled blood as well as mother's milk, draining unto death his own mother as well as several nurse maids.

It is unknown whether or not these tales are true.

It is known, however, that Stoke has lived several hundred years, and that he is utterly mad, deriving perverse pleasure from flaying people alive and impaling them. It is also said that he performs unspeakable rites upon the corpses, and perhaps is involved in necromancy.

Petal

A slender, damman Warrow, Petal is three feet high and has black hair and eyes of amber gold.

Before he was slain by Baron Stoke, Petal's sire was a travelling entertainer, juggling, walking the high wire, throwing knives, and performing other acts of entertainment. Petal lost her mother to the plague when she was but a wee youngling.

The damman became most proficient in throwing her sire's knives, and Tomlin's mother taught the child to walk a tightrope.

Petal was 20 when her sire and Tomlin's sire and dam were slain by Baron Stoke. Apparently, Stoke made her witness his mad act.

Her full name is Petal Downtuft.

MAGICAL REALMS

☐ **KING OF THE SCEPTER'D ISLE—A Fantasy Novel by Michael Greatex Coney.** King Arthur watches with dread as deadly betrayal could spell the end of Camelot . . . until Fang, the most courageous of the Gnomes, joins forces with Arthur and the beautiful Dedo Nyneve to manipulate history in a final confrontation of wills and worlds. "Spirited, zestful . . . truly magical."—*Booklist* (450426—$4.50)

☐ **SUNDER, ECLIPSE AND SEED—A Fantasy Novel by Elyse Guttenberg.** Even as Calyx struggles with her new-found power of prophecy, her skills are tested when the evil Edishu seeks to conquer Calyx and her people through their own dreams. (450469—$4.95)

☐ **WIZARD'S MOLE—A Fantasy Novel by Brad Strickland.** Can the politics of magic and the magic of advertising defeat the Great Dark One's bid for ultimate power? (450566—$4.50)

☐ **MOONWISE by Greer Ilene Gilman.** It was Ariane and Sylvie's own creation, a wondrous imaginary realm—until the power of magic became terrifyingly real. (450949—$4.95)

☐ **THE LAST UNICORN by Peter S. Beagle.** One of the most beloved tales in the annals of fantasy—the spellbinding saga of a creature out of legend on a quest beyond time. (450523—$6.95)

☐ **THE HAWK'S GRAY FEATHER: *A book of the Keltiad* by Patricia Kennealy.** The opening volume of this magnificent trilogy recaptures all the wonder of the Arthurian legend. "Highly recommended . . . a successful blend of magic and myth."—*Library Journal* (450531—$4.95)

Buy them at your local

bookstore or use coupon

on next page for ordering.

FLIGHTS OF FANTASY